Frank Muir

Illustrated by Joseph Wright

First published 1986 by A & C Black (Publishers) Ltd
35 Bedford Row, London WC1R 4JH
Text copyright © 1986 Frank Muir
Illustrations copyright © 1986 Joseph Wright
All rights reserved.
Photoset in Garamond by Tunbridge Wells Typesetting Services
Printed in Portugal by Resopal

British Library Cataloguing in Publication Data
Muir, Frank
What-a-Mess has supper.
I. Title II. Wright, Joseph, 1947-
823'.914 [J] PZ7
ISBN 0-7136-2861-8

A & C BLACK · LONDON

If somebody had looked over the back hedge on that summer's evening they would have seen the Sultan of Zanzibar, wearing an enormous turban and a moth-eaten fur coat, sitting on top of the compost heap.

A closer look, though, would have revealed that it was not really the Sultan of Zanzibar. It was a small, fat Afghan puppy, named Prince Amir of Kinjan but called What-a-Mess, and his coat was not moth-eaten but merely scruffy and full of the usual tangle of twigs, rose clippings, burrs and other assorted bits of dead nature. And the puppy was not wearing a vast turban but balancing on his head a "Sleepytime Hygienic Canine Bean Bag".

He was wearing the bean bag because he saw it when he was mooching around the house and put it on his head for something to do.

What-a-Mess was bored stiff.

He started playing a game of I-Spy with himself. He got A for Ant and B for Bird and then could not find a C. A mouse peeped out of a hole and he claimed C for Cow but it was no fun cheating himself so he stopped playing.

"Just because I ate my basket!" he muttered to himself. "Made to stay at home all day while the family and my mother go out and enjoy themselves."

And he was hungry, too.

Like all puppies, What-a-Mess needed lots of food, often, to keep his fat little tummy firm and happy, and all that remained in the house to eat was half a jug of milk at the back of the fridge. What-a-Mess dearly loved milk. He was saving the half-jugful for his supper.

He glanced up at the bean bag, which had begun to settle round his ears.

"I hate you, rotten bean bag!" he said.

He jumped down from the compost heap, broke into a run, and gave a twist of his head in the direction of the horizon.

The bean bag sailed through the air about six feet and landed with a light thud among the geraniums.

"Oy!" said a tiny, squeaky voice.

What-a-Mess dashed over and lifted the bean bag. Under it, on her back, tiny pink feet waving as she struggled to turn right way up, was a small hedgehog. "Hello!" said the hedgehog. "It's me!"

"Cynthia!" said What-a-Mess. "I *am* sorry! I was trying to throw my bean bag away!"

"No damage done." said Cynthia, scrambling up. "My fault for not dodging. I was looking for grubs to eat. What's wrong with the bean bag?"

"Everything, Cynthia. Look, you're much cleverer than I am.

Please help me get rid of it. It's too light to *throw* very far . . ."
Cynthia thought for a moment. "Tried the dustbin?" she said.
Off they went to the dustbin, Cynthia running to keep up.

The dustbin was nearly full. What-a-Mess had a quick rummage to make sure there was no edible food in it then the two of them tried to stuff the bean bag into the dustbin.

It was like trying to squeeze a haggis into an egg-cup.

"The dustbin's too small." said What-a-Mess.

Cynthia thought a moment. "Let's post it," she said.

They dragged the bag across the road. Cynthia stood on What-a-Mess's head and tried to feed the bean bag through the slot of the postbox, a little at a time. She got some of it through but such an enormous balloon of beans was left that there was obviously no hope.

"The bag's too fat," said What-a-Mess. "Let's empty out some of the beans."

They trundled the bag back across the road and into the drawing-room. What-a-Mess made a tear in it with his teeth and jumped down heavily on it from the back of the sofa.

Tiny balls of white plastic flew out. Millions and millions of them. Light as thistledown, they filled the drawing-room like a snowstorm and stuck to everything, the curtains, the carpet, the walls.

What-a-Mess ran around frantically, trying to gather them in but the plastic beans dodged round him, floating into the air when he tried to pick them up.

"Look at the mess!" he wailed. "And the family will be back soon!"

"Tell you what," said the little hedgehog. "Use *me!*"

She gave a twitch and rolled herself into a ball, her spines standing out like needles.

The puppy rolled Cynthia across the carpet and the curtains. The little hedgehog's sharp spines impaled the plastic pellets and held them firmly. When Cynthia was full, What-a-Mess slid the beans off her and put them back into the bean bag. Soon there was not a bean to be seen.

"How can I thank you enough!" said the grateful puppy.

"Well," said the hedgehog, "I *should* have been out looking for food. Have you such a thing as a little milk for me to drink?"

What-a-Mess was very good. Not for a moment did he show that he was saving the milk for his own supper. He poured it out for Cynthia and watched, forcing a smile, as she drank every drop. She left, fed.

Then he saw headlights and heard a car tooting. He leaped in the air and ran twice round the garden and jumped up and barked as the family and his mother returned home at long last.

When the family had trooped upstairs, the puppy's mother said to him, "Have you been a good boy all day? If so, we've brought you back a little present."

"I've been almost *perfect!*" said What-a-Mess.

She led him into the room where they slept.

There, in his corner, stood a brand-new sleeping-basket.

In a few minutes his tired mother was in a deep sleep but the puppy was wide awake with excitement. The new cushion under him was plump and wonderfully comfortable. The high sides of the basket were perfect to settle against.

The newly-varnished wickerwork, an inch from his nose, gave off the nicest of smells.

The puppy gave the edge of the basket the tiniest of nibbles. It was crunchy and had a very agreeable taste: half-biscuit, half-toffee. He took a larger bite . . .

What-a-Mess had supper.